To Mo and Paul,
who know how to be them

First U.S. edition 2020
First published by Otter-Barry Books (U.K.) 2020

Library of Congress Catalog Card Number pending
ISBN 978-1-5362-1470-3

19 20 21 22 23 24 TLF 10 9 8 7 6 5 4 3 2 1

Printed in Dongguan, Guangdong, China

This book was hand-lettered by the author-illustrator.
The illustrations were done in brush and ink and rendered digitally.

Candlewick Press
99 Dover Street
Somerville, Massachusetts 02144

visit us at www.candlewick.com

Only a Tree
knows how to be a tree

Mary Murphy

CANDLEWICK PRESS

A tree has leaves
that turn sunshine
into tree food.
Amazing!

Later,
the leaves
change color

and

twirl

to

the

ground.

A tree gives shelter.
It can be a home.

Only a tree knows
how to be a tree.

Birds build
nests for homes.

They sing
different songs,

and their babies
hatch from eggs.

Best of all,
they can fly.

Only a bird knows
how to be a bird.

Dogs are our friends.
They play with us and love us.

They wag their tail and move their ears to show us how they feel. They flick water into their mouth to drink.

I can't do that, but then only a dog knows how to be a dog.

Water has no color,
but you can see it.
It makes rivers and oceans,
clouds and rain and snow.

Fish live in water.
They flash like jewels.

Everyone needs water.
Only water knows
how to be water.

Only fish know how to be fish.

Earth is where we live,
with all the plants,
animals, oceans,
mountains, and rivers.

Earth spins around
and gives us day and night.
It tilts through the year
and gives us seasons.

There are countless stars
in the universe
and many, many planets.

But Earth is our home.
Only Earth knows how to be Earth.

Every comet,

flower,

cat,

and beetle,

every cloud,

frog,

stone,

and duck,

every mountain,

river,

and deer is different.

Every tree is different.

And they are all the only ones
who know how to be them.

As for people, there are billions of us.

We eat and talk,
sing and walk.

We work. We play. We tell stories.

Every person
has their own thoughts
in their head
and their own feelings
in their heart.

Every single person is different.
And only they know how to be them.

Only I know how to be me.

And only you know how to be you.